The Narrow Escapes of Davy Crockett

From a Bear, a Boa Constrictor, a Hoop Snake, an Elk, an Owl, Eagles, Rattlesnakes, Wildcats, Trees, Tornadoes, a Sinking Ship, and Niagara Falls

by ARIANE DEWEY

A MULBERRY PAPERBACK BOOK
NEW YORK

AUTHOR'S NOTE: MOST OF THESE STORIES AND SOME
OF THE ORIGINAL LANGUAGE COME FROM THE CROCKETT ALMANACS,
PUBLISHED BETWEEN 1835 AND 1856

Watercolor paints and a black line were used for the full color art.
The text type is Bookman. Copyright © 1990 by Ariane Dewey. All rights reserved.
No part of this book may be reproduced or utilized in any form or by any means, electronic
or mechanical, including photocopying, recording or by any information storage and retrieval
system, without permission in writing from the Publisher, Greenwillow Books, a division of
William Morrow and Company, Inc., 1350 Avenue of the Americas, New York, NY 10019.
Printed in the United States of America   First Mulberry Edition, 1993.
1   3   5   7   9   10   8   6   4   2

Library of Congress Cataloging-in-Publication Data
Dewey, Ariane.
The narrow escapes of Davy Crockett / by Ariane Dewey.—1st Mulberry ed.
p.   cm.
Summary: Recounts the wild adventures of Davy Crockett, including
his tangles with a wrestling bear, eagles that wish to pull out his hair,
and an alligator he rides up Niagara Falls.
ISBN 0-688-12269-8
1. Crockett, Davy, 1786-1836—Juvenile fiction.   [1. Crockett, Davy 1786-
1836—Fiction.   2. Tall tales.]   I. Title.
[PZ7.D5228Nar   1993]
[E]—dc20   92-24586   CIP   AC

FOR **K**IT

*T*here never was anyone like Davy
Crockett. By the time he was eight years
old he weighed two hundred pounds with
his shoes off, his feet clean, and his
stomach empty.

When he grew up he could run faster, jump higher, squat lower, dive deeper, stay down longer, and come up drier than any man in Tennessee. He could swim like an eel and carry a keelboat on his back.

WHOA! He could stare down a streak of lightning without blinking, or pull a rainbow out of the sky. He had the surest rifle and the ugliest dog anywhere. He just couldn't be beat!

*D*avy loved danger, and what he loved next best was telling about it.

His favorite story was about the time he was caught from behind in a ferociously tight embrace. A great bear was hugging him like a brother, but with no love in it. The bear licked Davy's neck to feel where to sink in its teeth.

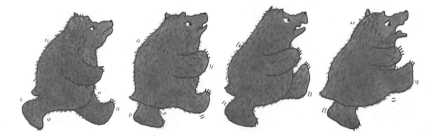

Now that made Davy as mad as a pea
on a hot frying pan. His feet went into
action, kicking that bear in places it
didn't know it had.

They fell and rolled THUMP into a
dead tree which toppled over, knocking
them senseless.

Something shrieked
like one hundred
sawmills.
Davy jumped
about
seven
feet,
though
he didn't
stop to
measure.

The bear went
one way
and he went
the other.
It wasn't
the fastest
he'd ever run,
but he
wasn't
walking.

Pretty soon his curiosity slowed him down. He stuffed moss in his ears and crept back.

Confound it! There sat an OWL.

✳ EXTRA! EXTRA! ✳

Davy Crockett FRIGHTENED BY AN OWL

How mortifying!

He let out a roar that spun the owl around and carried it off. The owl hasn't been heard from since, but that wasn't the end of the bear.

One spring morning Davy heard a
racket coming from inside a tree.
How odd, he thought. He climbed up
to have a look. Crash! He fell in.
The tree was hollow.

Luckily he landed on something soft.
Then it growled. Drat! He'd woken a
bear from its winter nap.

"Hello, stranger," he said. But it wasn't
a stranger. It was the hugging bear.

It took one look at Davy and
scrambled up the hollow trunk. Davy
clamped his teeth on its tail. They came
out of that tree like a cannonball. The
bear was sore behind, and fled before
Davy could thank it for the ride!

*D*avy was exhausted, so he sat down, rested his head in the fork of a young tree, and fell asleep. He was awakened by something pulling at his hair. He thought he was being scalped. He tried to get up, but his head was stuck.

He bellowed and swore and begged for a fair fight. But his tormentor wouldn't stop. Davy felt like a gone sucker.

"Eagles are tearing your hair out to build their nests," a girl's voice said calmly as she chased them away.

Then she reached into a rattlesnake's hole, brought out a handful of snakes, and tied them into a rope. She fastened the rope to one of the trunks and pulled. Davy's head popped free, and he got a look at her.

WHOOW! She was a regular steamboat. Her arms were as long and strong as roof beams. She said her name was Sally Ann Thunder Ann Whirlwind. Davy fell in love right then and there. He escorted her home and threatened to come calling.

24

He waited till the next day. When
he got within three miles of her house
he hollered Will You Marry Me?

His voice came through the woods like a tornado. It sounded so good that she said yes and they hitched up.

One cold night, after Sally Ann had gone to bed, Davy was sitting by the fire with Mortal Brown talking about nothing much. All at once a monstrous great wildcat bounced in through the window.

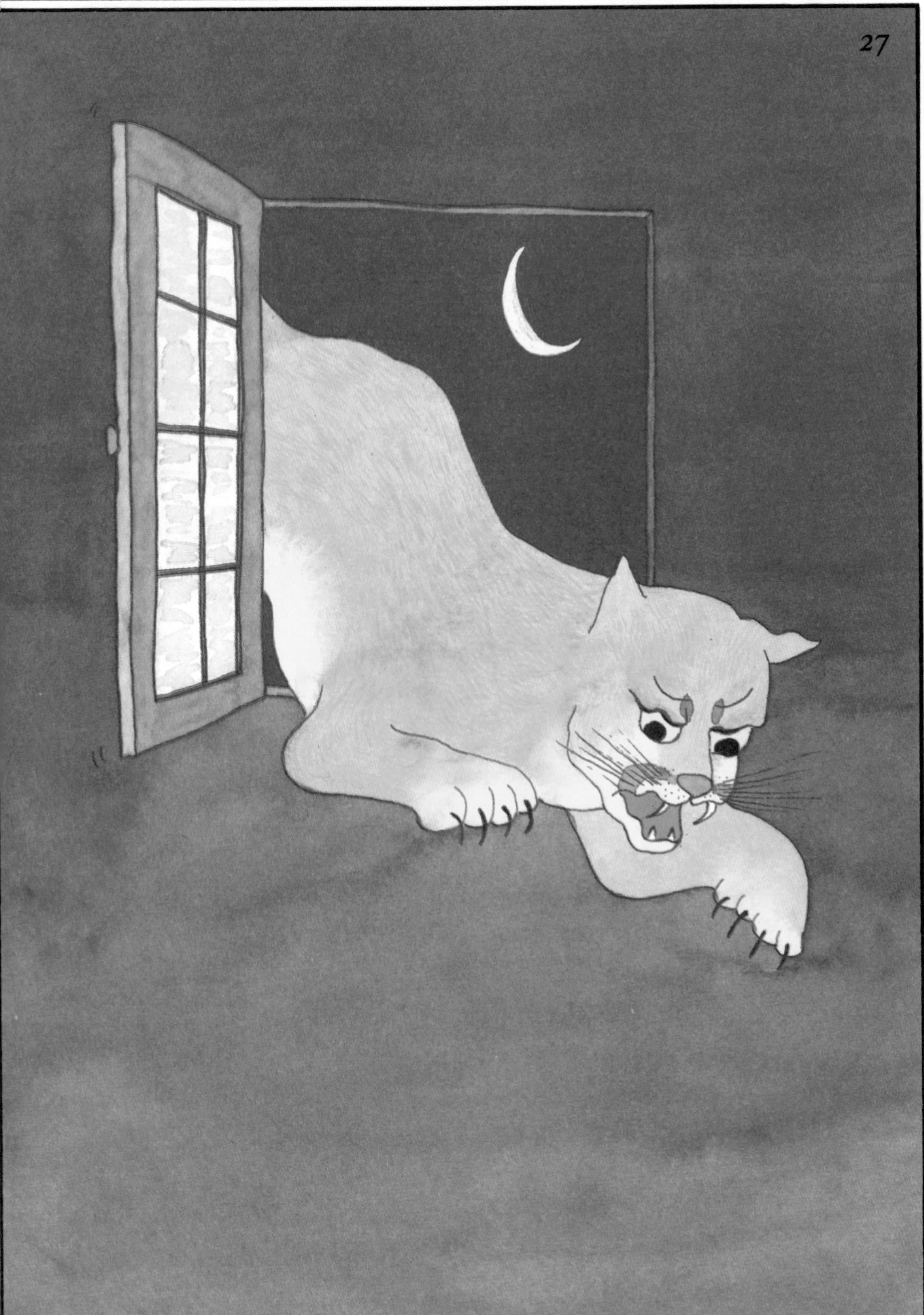

It crouched down, wagged its tail, and rolled its eyes. It couldn't decide who to eat first. Mortal and Davy sat as still as two rotten stumps in a fog.

"What should we do?" Mortal whispered.

"Seems likely one or the other of us will be chewed up before we're a minute older," Davy replied.

"We could run away while the panther eats your wife," Mortal suggested.

Now that made Davy boil over.
He pounced on that scoundrel like a
rampaging alligator. The wildcat sprang,
too. The tussle was a tangle. Davy
bounced the panther back out the
window. Then he came down on Mortal
like the Mississippi on a sand bar.
Mortal was as raw as an oak with its
bark off when he left. Sally Ann never
even woke up.

Davy knew he was a goner for sure the time something sneaked up and wound itself around him. A huge boa constrictor glared at him with evil red eyes and opened its jaws ridiculously wide.

Davy tried to grin back, but the snake
was cramping his breathing. He thought
he'd better cut out before it crushed him
into Crockett jelly. Big Butcher, his knife,
was stuck in his belt. He wriggled and
twisted to turn the blade out. When the
boa squeezed, Big Butcher sliced right
through it.

Once Davy cut the rattles off a dead
rattlesnake. They'd make a nice toy for
his daughter, Rockett Ann.

But when Davy jiggled them, the
sound made another rattler mad. It stuck
its tail in its mouth, turned into a hoop,
and rolled straight at Davy.

He ran. But the faster he ran, the
louder the rattles rattled and the angrier
the snake became. Davy threw the rattles
at the snake, who caught them in his
poisonous jaws, crushing them to bits.

Davy headed for home as fast as dry
dust in a hurricane.

*T*hen there was that trip he and Ben
Hardin took on a Mississippi steamer.
They were talking politics about as loud
as low thunder when there was a distant
rumble.

"Hello, here comes a storm," said the
captain.

"Bah! It's only the echo of our voices,"
said Davy.

But the sound got louder, the water
began to squirm, and the boat started
playing seesaw. The trees walked out
of the ground on their roots. Houses
splintered, and some people appeared
to be going up to heaven feet first.

"Unpleasant weather," said Ben.

Just then a streak of lightning flashed
by. Davy grabbed hold and they jumped
on. He and Ben left in an astonishing
hurry.

*B*ut Davy's most memorable ride was
up Niagara Falls on the back of his
pet alligator. Everyone swore he'd
drown. But he tickled the alligator
with his toe, twisted its tail around
himself, and held his nose.
Then they walked up that
hill of water as slick
as you please.

Davy was running for Congress.
On election day he set out to vote.
A catamount frowned down at him from
a tall oak. Davy climbed up to share its
point of view. It put its jaws close to his
ear, as if to pass on some advice. Just
then the branch broke. Davy landed on
an elk. And who knows where the cat
hit down?

The elk bolted and bucked all the way to the Little Fork of Great Skunk's Liver River. That's where the election was. If Davy did win a seat in Congress, he'd be too sore to sit in it.

"Hurray for Crockett!" the people cheered. The elk reared and threw Davy right into the middle of the crowd.

"Sure is different how you people *run for office*," said a fellow from down east.

"WHOOP!" Davy shouted as he
jumped on a stump. "Vote for me! I'm
a real screamer. I can outtalk any
congressman without taking a breath."
Davy stood there all day, spouting
stories like a volcano.

He was just starting on another one
when Sally Ann whistled up a whirlwind
to carry his words away.

"Stop running for Congress and come
home for supper!" she demanded. This
time Davy knew better than to try and
escape.

The next day Davy heard he'd won the election. He and Sally Ann set right out for Washington. And there Davy Crockett and his stories became more and more famous.